FROM
UNCLE LIONEL
& ANTIE MARILYN.

Barbara Reid

# Baby's First Treasury

## Scholastic Canada Ltd.
Toronto  New York  London  Auckland  Sydney
Mexico City  New Delhi  Hong Kong  Buenos Aires

The illustrations for this book were made with Plasticine,
shaped and pressed onto illustration board.

Photography by Ian Crysler

Library and Archives Canada Cataloguing in Publication

Reid, Barbara, 1957-
[Works. Selections]
Baby's first treasury / Barbara Reid.

Contents:  Welcome baby -- Read me a book -- Sing a song of
Mother Goose -- Zoe's year.
ISBN 978-1-4431-4852-8 (hardback)

I. Reid, Barbara, 1957- Welcome baby.  II. Reid, Barbara, 1957-
Read me a book.  III. Reid, Barbara, 1957- Sing a song of Mother Goose.
IV. Reid, Barbara, 1957- Zoe's year.  VI. Title.

PS8585.E4484A6 2016           jC813'.54           C2016-900655-7

6  5  4  3  2  1      Printed in Malaysia 108     16  17  18  19  20

# Table of Contents

*For YOU!*
—*B.R.*

# Welcome, Baby

Welcome, baby, welcome!
All the world is new,
And all the world is waiting
To be introduced to you.

4

You will be our sunshine,
We'll be your biggest fans,

We'll tell you all our stories,

You're part of all our plans.

We can spend a noisy morning
And a quiet afternoon,

Play pat-a-cake and peek-a-boo,
And fly you to the moon.

# We'll climb the highest mountains,

We'll sail the seven seas,

Then stop and smell the roses,

And listen to the trees.

We'll sing and dance
and laugh and cry,

We'll hold you close,

And let you fly.

Welcome, baby, welcome!
All the world is new,
And we can't wait to celebrate
And share it all with you.

*To Mum and Dad.*
*— B.R.*

# Read Me a Book

# Tell me
# a story,

# Read me
# a book,

# Bounce me
# a poem,

Let's take
a look.

41

# Read around
# the garden,

# Upstairs
# and down,

Underneath
the covers,

47

# Read around the town.

49

# Tell it
# one more time,

# Pick out
# something new,

53

# The very best beginning is . . .

to read a book
with you!

57

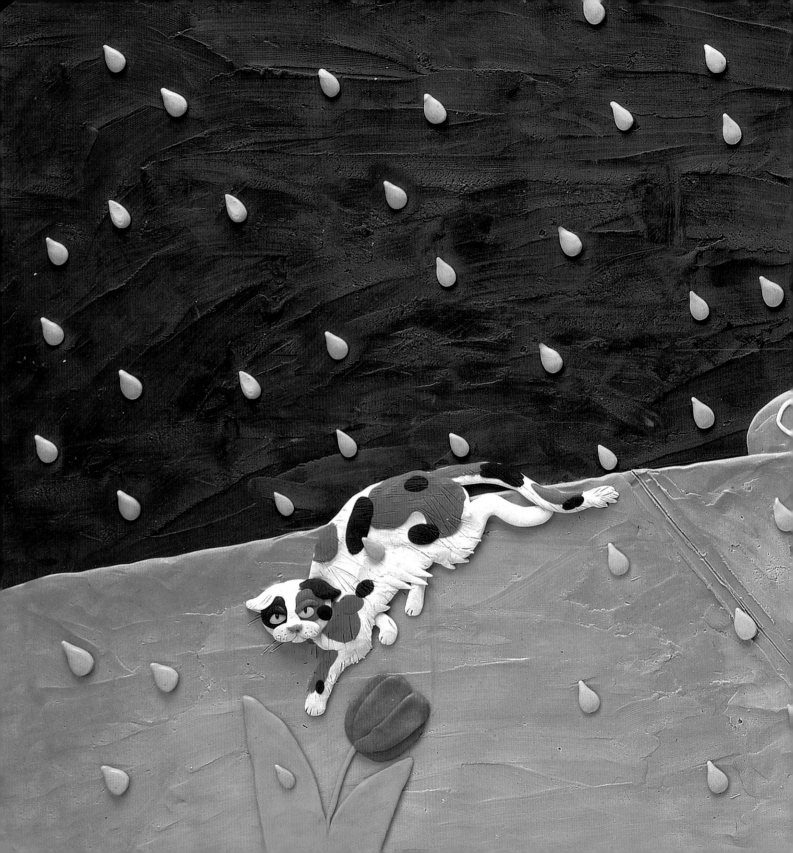

# Zoe's Rainy Day

**Where is Zoe going?**

Walking in the rain

Wet umbrellas

Muddy puddles

Zoe's clean again!

69

Zoe's Sunny Day

Where is Zoe going?

Playing in the park

Picnic lunch

76

Wading pool

Home before it's dark.

# Zoe's Windy Day

Where is Zoe going?

**Swinging in the breeze**

Hungry squirrels

Rosy cheeks

**More hot chocolate, please!**

# Zoe's Snowy Day

Where is Zoe going?

# Riding on her sled

# Big hill

100

Skating rink

Snowy dreams in bed.

*To W.H. for all the fun!*
*— B.R.*

# BARBARA REID

## Sing a Song of
# MOTHER
# GOOSE

## Sing a Song

Sing a song of sixpence,
A pocket full of rye;
Four and twenty blackbirds
Baked in a pie!

When the pie was opened
The birds began to sing;
Wasn't that a dainty dish
To set before the king?

# Jack and Jill

Jack and Jill
Went up the hill,
To fetch a pail of water;
Jack fell down
And broke his crown,
And Jill came tumbling after.

# Hey Diddle, Diddle

Hey diddle diddle,
The cat and the fiddle,
The cow jumped over the moon;
The little dog laughed
To see such sport,
And the dish ran away
with the spoon.

## Ladybug

Ladybug, ladybug,
    fly away home!
Your house is on fire,
    your children all gone;
All but one,
    and her name is Ann,
And she crept under
    the pudding pan.

# Mary Had a Little Lamb

Mary had a little lamb,
Its fleece was white as snow;
And everywhere that Mary went
The lamb was sure to go.

It followed her to school one day,
Which was against the rules;
It made the children laugh and play
To see a lamb at school.

# Humpty Dumpty

Humpty Dumpty
  sat on a wall,
Humpty Dumpty
  had a great fall;
All the king's horses
  and all the king's men
Couldn't put Humpty
  together again.

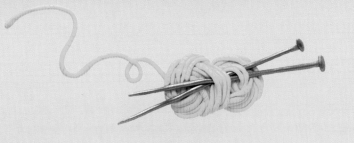

# Baa, Baa, Black Sheep

Baa, baa, black sheep,
Have you any wool?
Yes, sir, yes, sir,
Three bags full;
One for the master,
One for the dame,
And one for the little boy
Who lives down the lane.

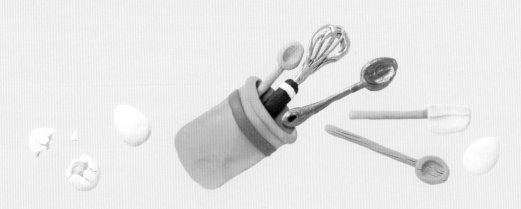

## Pat-a-Cake

Pat-a-cake, pat-a-cake,
Baker's man!
Bake me a cake
As fast as you can.
Pat it, and prick it,
And mark it with B,
Put it in the oven
For baby and me.

# Pussy Cat, Pussy Cat

Pussy cat, pussy cat,
Where have you been?
I've been to London
To visit the queen.
Pussy cat, pussy cat,
What did you there?
I frightened a little mouse
Under her chair.

124

# Rock-a-bye Baby

Rock-a-bye baby,
On the tree top,
When the wind blows
The cradle will rock;
When the bough breaks
The cradle will fall,
And down will come baby,
Cradle, and all.

# Rain

Rain, rain, go away,
Come again another day;
Little Johnny wants to play.

# Little Miss Muffet

Little Miss Muffet
Sat on a tuffet,
Eating her curds and whey;
There came a big spider,
Who sat down beside her
And frightened Miss Muffet away.

# Hickory, Dickory, Dock

Hickory, dickory, dock,
The mouse ran up the clock.
The clock struck one,
The mouse ran down,
Hickory, dickory, dock.

# Twinkle, Twinkle, Little Star

Twinkle, twinkle, little star,
How I wonder what you are!
Up above the world so high,
Like a diamond in the sky.

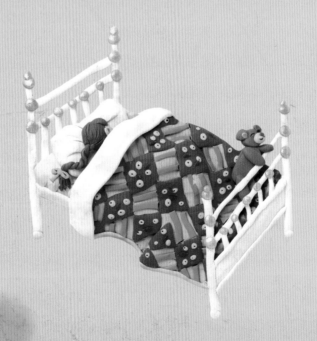